OLD BLACK FLY

JIM AYLESWORTH

**Illustrations by
STEPHEN GAMMELL**

Henry Holt and Company · New York

To my brother Bill,
a legendary swatter of flies,
with love.   —J. A.

Henry Holt and Company, LLC
Publishers since 1866
115 West 18th Street
New York, New York 10011

Henry Holt is a registered
trademark of Henry Holt and Company, LLC

Library of Congress Cataloging-in-Publication Data
Aylesworth, Jim.
Old black fly / by Jim Aylesworth;
illustrated by Stephen Gammell.
Summary: Rhyming text and illustrations follow a mischievous
old black fly through the alphabet as he has a very busy bad
day landing where he should not be.
[1. Flies—Fiction. 2. Alphabet. 3. Stories in rhyme.]
I. Gammell, Stephen, ill. II. Title.
PZ8.3.A9501 1991 [E]—dc20 91-26825

First published in hardcover in 1992 by Henry Holt and Company
First Owlet paperback edition, 1995

Printed in the United States of America on acid-free paper. ∞
ISBN 0-8050-1401-2 (hardcover)
20 19 18 17 16 15 14 13 12 11
ISBN 0-8050-3924-4 (paperback)
20 19 18 17 16 15 14 13 12

Old black fly's been
buzzin' around,
buzzin' around,
buzzin' around.
Old black fly's been
buzzin' around,
And he's had a very
busy bad day.

He ate on the crust
of the **A**pple pie.

He bothered the **B**aby
and made her cry.
Shoo fly!
Shoo fly!
Shooo.

He coughed on the Cookies with the chocolate bits.

He drove the **D**og
nearly out of his wits.
Shoo fly!
Shoo fly!
Shooo.

He frolicked on the **E**ggs
for the birthday cake.

He licked up the **F**rosting,
for goodness sake.
Shoo fly!
Shoo fly!
Shooo.

He danced on the edge
of the **G**arbage sack.

He got sweet **H**oney
on his dirty back.
        Shoo fly!
        Shoo fly!
        Shooo.

He hid in the Ivy
by the kitchen sink.

He stole some Jelly
as quick as a wink.
Shoo fly!
Shoo fly!
Shooo.

He played on the **K**eys
by the kitchen door.

He lit on the **L**ist
for the grocery store.
Shoo fly!
Shoo fly!
Shooo.

chocolate
eggs
apples
olive oil
honey
milk
salami
jelly
noodles

He lapped up the **M**ilk
in poor kitty's bowl.

He nibbled on **N**oodles
in the casserole.
Shoo fly!
Shoo fly!
Shooo.

He crawled in the spills
from the **O**live oil can.

He pestered the **P**arrot
on her stand.

Shoo fly!
Shoo fly!
Shooo.

He snoozed on the Quilt
on Gramma's bed.

He rode the red **R**ibbon
on her head.
Shoo fly!
Shoo fly!
Shooo.

He sniffed the **S**alami
that sister sliced.

He ran around her Teacup
once or twice.
Shoo fly!
Shoo fly!
Shooo.

He slept on the stack
of clean **U**nderwear.

He played on the **V**ase
by the velvet chair.
Shoo fly!
Shoo fly!
Shooo.

He dozed on the **W**indow
in the summer heat.

He made a little **X**
with his front feet.
  Shoo fly!
  Shoo fly!
  Shooo.

He buzzed about the **Y**arn
in Mama's lap.

He landed on her table,
flap flip flap.

Zzzzz Zzz!
Zzzz Zzz!
Zzzzz.

Old black fly's done
buzzin' around,
buzzin' around,
buzzin' around.
Old black fly's done
buzzin' around,
and he won't be bad
no more.